ONE
LAST JOB

ONE LAST JOB

SEAN RODMAN

ORCA BOOK PUBLISHERS

Published in Canada and the United States
in 2022 by Orca Book Publishers.
orcabook.com

Library and Archives Canada Cataloguing in Publication
Title: One last job / Sean Rodman.
Names: Rodman, Sean, 1972- author.
Description: Series statement: Orca anchor
Identifiers: Canadiana (print) 20210166746 |
Canadiana (ebook) 20210166746 | ISBN 9781459828605 (softcover) |
ISBN 9781459828438 (PDF) | ISBN 9781459828445 (EPUB)
Classification: LCC PS8635.O355 O54 2022 | DDC jc813/.6—dc23

Library of Congress Control Number: 2021934074

Summary: In this high-interest accessible novel for teen readers,
Michael convinces his grandfather, a retired cat burglar,
to help him steal back a valuable necklace.

Orca Book Publishers is committed to reducing the consumption
of nonrenewable resources in the production of our books. We make
every effort to use materials that support a sustainable future.

Orca Book Publishers gratefully acknowledges the support
for its publishing programs provided by the following agencies:
the Government of Canada, the Canada Council for the Arts and
the Province of British Columbia through the BC Arts Council
and the Book Publishing Tax Credit.

Cover artwork by Getty Images/Image Source
and Ella Collier
Design by Ella Collier
Edited by Tanya Trafford
Author photo by BK Studios Photographers

Printed and bound in Canada.

25 24 23 22 • 1 2 3 4

To Jasmine and Isaac,

who enjoy a good heist.

Chapter One

The robbery happens fast. We never even see it coming.

Gramps and I are sitting on his old green couch. We are watching TV. Taking turns answering the questions that the game-show host asks. I am almost always right. Particularly anything to do with sports or geography. When the show finishes, Gramps turns to me.

"When did you get so smart?" he says. "You act like some dumb tough guy around your friends, Mikey. I swear that big brain of yours is going to take you—"

There is a crash of glass from the back door near the kitchen. I stand up, my plate clattering to the floor.

Then the burglar is right in front of us. His face is completely hidden. A red bandanna over his mouth. Mirrored sunglasses across his eyes. A black Yankees ball cap pulled down low on his head.

He holds a dull gray pistol in one hand and levels it at my chest. Then jerks it toward Gramps. Then back to me. I slowly put up my hands and ease back down onto the couch.

My heartbeat thuds in my ears. I can feel my chest tighten. This kind of stuff happens in our neighborhood occasionally. It never ends well.

Gramps has a heart condition too. Something like this could trigger an attack. My mom told me that I have to give him pills if that happens. But I've never actually done it.

The burglar shouts something through the red bandanna covering his mouth. I can't tell what he is saying. Neither can Gramps.

"I'm sorry," says Gramps politely. "You'll have to repeat that."

I tear my eyes away from the gun to look at Gramps. How can he be so calm? Gramps blinks slowly behind his thick glasses. He coughs softly.

The burglar turns his head a little to the side. He's a skinny guy. For a second he looks like a weird bird with his head like that. Gramps clears his throat and tries again.

"I can't understand you. Look, I guess it's my fault. I'm not wearing my hearing aids. But that rag over your mouth? It isn't helping. Maybe if you take it off?"

The burglar pauses. Thinks about it. Frustrated, he rips off the bandanna.

"This is a robbery!" he shouts again. Louder. Angrier. "Do not move a freakin' muscle!" He points with his gun for emphasis.

"That I understand," says Gramps. "And I won't move. It takes me half an hour to get up from this couch. You've got nothing to worry about."

Still, the burglar pulls out a couple of thick black plastic zip ties. Using them, he ties up Gramps and then me. The little plastic zip ties aren't enough to stop us. But they are enough to slow us down long enough for him to shoot us. If we are dumb enough to move. While he's tying us up, I study his face. He has a little cold sore on the edge of his lip. His breath smells like garlic.

Satisfied, the burglar stuffs the gun into the waistband of his jeans. Then he starts to search the one-room apartment. It won't take him long. The place is tiny. A single bed with a dresser next to it. A mini-kitchen with a mini-fridge. A desk. And a green couch, where we sit. All tied up.

The burglar pulls out a drawer from my grandpa's desk. He shakes it upside down. Papers and pens fall to the floor.

"You want some pencils?" says Gramps. "I've even got pens, if that's what you're looking for."

"Don't make him mad," I hiss at Gramps. The burglar ignores us and keeps on making a mess. He dumps a bunch of files out, papers flying everywhere. Then sweeps a stack of hardcover books from their shelves. He empties kitchen cabinets. Pots and pans clatter across the linoleum.

"He's not very good at this," says Gramps.

"Shut it!" roars the burglar, not looking at us. He's busy tossing clothes out of the dresser onto the floor.

Gramps lowers his voice and leans toward me. "Seriously, this guy is an amateur. And I should know."

Gramps has lived, as he puts it, an "adventurous life." He doesn't talk much about it, and neither do my parents. But I know he had a criminal career that ended with a couple of years in prison.

"How about I save us all some time?" says Gramps to the burglar. "There's twenty bucks in a pickle jar by the door. It's for the cleaning lady. Aside from that, you're not going to find anything here. I've got nothing to hide."

The burglar slowly stands up and turns around. He pulls an old wool sock out of the dresser. There is clearly something hidden inside the sock. Reaching in, he pulls it out. A small wooden box. The burglar sneers.

"Nothing to hide, huh?" he says and tilts open the lid. Gramps swears softly. The burglar lifts up a necklace. It's a thin silver chain with a teardrop-shaped pendant dangling at the end. It catches the light and sparkles like a drop of water.

"That's no good to you," says Gramps. "Seriously, take the money. Take the TV. Whatever. But leave that, all right?"

The burglar takes several steps toward us. "Naw. I'm taking it."

"Back off!" I yell. I spring from the couch, but the burglar gives me a sharp shove in the chest, sending me to the floor.

Suddenly my grandfather's watery blue eyes turn hard and focused. His voice rattles like a rake over gravel.

"You are making a mistake, son. Leave my grandson alone. Leave the necklace where you found it. Walk away. Take the money by the door. I won't call the cops. Final offer."

The burglar leans down over Gramps. He dangles the necklace in front of the old man.

"You really trying to scare me?" He lunges at Gramps suddenly. Expecting him to flinch. Trying to frighten him. But Gramps doesn't even blink.

"No," says Gramps. "I'm just giving you fair warning. Steal that necklace, hurt my family, and you'll pay." For a moment the burglar hesitates. Then his lips curl into a sneer, and he shakes his head. Then he walks toward the front door. As he passes me lying on the floor, he swings a boot at my chest. The air whooshes out of my lungs, and I gasp for air. The burglar grabs the pickle jar by the door and then slips out the door.

It doesn't take long for me to cut the zip ties off my wrists and free Gramps. I reach for my cell phone.

"Don't do that," says Gramps. He hasn't moved from the couch since the burglar left. He's just sitting there. Rubbing his wrists. Thinking.

"Don't tell the cops," he adds. "And don't tell your parents. Don't tell anyone. We're going to handle this. You and me."

That's when Mom walks in.

Chapter Two

Mom slowly scans the apartment. Takes in the clothes scattered across the floor. The papers and books tossed everywhere.

"What happened here?" she asks carefully.

"Rats," says Gramps. He flashes me a quick look. It's cold and hard. Like a wolf about to pounce. Clearly, I better play along. Then his eyes soften as he looks over at my mom. "They were terrifying. Big ones."

She raises an eyebrow. "Rats?"

"Yup," I lie. "Gramps saw a couple of rats, and we were trying to catch them." I can't look her in the face. I pick up a big pot from the kitchen floor instead. I place it carefully on the windowsill.

"One rat means a family of rats," says Gramps. "You know these old buildings. I didn't want to call anyone. I figured it could be part of Mikey's summer job. You know, part of taking care of me."

"This isn't what I had in mind," says Mom, distracted. She is still taking in the apartment. It looks like a bomb has just gone off. With ground zero being Gramps's underwear drawer.

"I thought Michael would take you for

walks," she continues. "Make sure you took your heart medicine. Not chase rats around your apartment."

This was Mom's plan to keep me off the streets for the rest of the summer. Like I said, our neighborhood isn't the best. My mom's an ER nurse. Dad is out of the picture. So there's not much parental supervision right now. I'd ended up hanging out with some pretty sketchy characters. Like Tank. Same age as me. Twice my size. Half the common sense. Tank always seemed to be lurking on street corners. Always at the center of things, good or bad.

Then Gramps had started to have health issues. He'd forget to take his medicine. On his eightieth birthday, Gramps had a small heart attack. Angina, my mom called it. He ended up in the ER. Mom freaked out when she saw Gramps being wheeled in on a stretcher. That's when she came up with a plan. She'd pay me to look after Gramps until school started in the fall.

So now I'm getting paid to hang out with my grandfather. My duties are pretty basic. Take the old man for walks. Make sure he eats his vegetables. Measure out a handful of different pills for him every day. Keep him and myself out of trouble.

Except my duties now included lying to my mom.

"Mikey's been doing an excellent job," says Gramps. "I've never been healthier. And now my place is free of rats, thanks to my boy here." I start picking up books, sliding them in batches back on the shelves. "Look at him go. He'll have the place tidied up in no time."

Mom narrows her eyes. She stands there, hands on hips, in her blue medical scrubs. I don't think she's buying it.

"I don't know what you two are really up to," she says. "But as long as you're both healthy and happy, I guess it doesn't matter what games you're playing." She walks over and gives Gramps a hug.

"You've gotten into more than enough trouble in your lifetime," she says to Gramps. "And remember, we're trying to keep you healthy and Michael out of trouble. Be good." Mom kisses Gramps on his wrinkled forehead. The guilt of not telling her the truth burns in my gut. But Gramps keeps shooting me that wolf look. So I keep my mouth shut.

Chapter Three

After Mom leaves, I get back to tidying up. I spot a framed photo of Gramps and Grandma. It's their wedding picture. Gramps looks good in a black suit and tie. Grandma looks amazing. I look closer and see she is wearing the pendant necklace.

"That was Grandma's necklace? Why don't you want to tell Mom about this?

Or call the cops?" I ask Gramps. "You got robbed. It's not like it's your fault."

"Mikey, you know I did some bad things in the past, right? Stuff I regret. Stuff I went to prison for. One of those bad things? It involved that necklace."

"Oh. So you're saying you stole it," I say.

Gramps nods slowly. "Yeah. That necklace is worth a *lot* of money. If I call the cops, they might ask questions about where it came from. Even though it was a long time ago. Besides, I'm an ex-con. It's not like the police are going to work hard to help me out." He points at the photo. "But it's not about the money."

He pauses a moment before continuing.

"I stole that necklace because I wanted to impress your grandmother. I thought I needed something fancy to seal the deal."

"Did it work?" I pass the photo to him. He smiles at it.

"Well, she married me, so yeah, I guess it worked. We had a lot of happy years together." His face crinkles into a big smile. Then it fades. "But when I was in prison, your grandmother got cancer."

It's getting dark in the apartment. But I can see his cheeks are wet. Gramps cradles the picture in his hands.

"The whole time she was fading away, I was locked up. That necklace? That's all I have left of her now," he says quietly. "That's why I need to get it back."

After a moment Gramps looks up at me. "So you going to help me or what?"

This is not what my mom had in mind when she asked me to look after Gramps. But I can see how important this is to my grandfather.

"Yeah," I say. "Of course. But how can I help?"

"Let's start by figuring out who robbed us. Your mom is always saying that you hang with a bad crowd. You got a friend on the street who might know something?"

Chapter Four

I find Tank hanging out at the corner of Becker and Key Streets. The heart of the neighborhood. Right where he likes to be—in the center of things.

Tank is sitting on an old milk crate. He's a big guy, so the crate looks tiny underneath him. He has flipped over a couple of buckets to make homemade drums. He's hammering away on them as

I walk up to him. With a big flourish, he finishes his solo.

"Michael, my man!" Tank gives me a big grin. He spins a drumstick in one hand. "Haven't seen you around much. Where you been?"

"Oh, you know. Here and there." I move closer to Tank and lower my voice. "Listen, I need some advice."

"Advice?" Tank smiles even bigger. He shakes his head like he doesn't believe me. "You're the local genius. Always with your nose in a book. Smart enough to stay out of trouble. So what kind of advice you need from me?"

"My gramps got robbed last night. The guy took something important to him."

"Aw, sorry to hear that," says Tank. "Your grandfather was always good to me. Even when I was a punk to him. I owe him a few."

"He asked me to find the guy who did it."

It takes Tank a second to figure out what I'm asking for. "You want to find the guy who robbed your gramps?"

I shrug and nod. "Yeah."

"And what are you and Gramps going to do when you find him? Beat him up?" He looks me up and down. I know what he's seeing. I'm short. More bone than muscle. "No offense, but you two aren't Batman and Robin."

"Maybe I could buy it back from him?"

Tank snorts. He lifts an eyebrow. "That's the dumbest idea I've ever heard."

He launches into a rapid-fire drumroll on his buckets and closes his eyes.

I guess this is a dead end. I turn to leave.

But then the drums stop.

"Hold on, Michael." Tank sighs. "I know you. You're going to keep asking around. Until you get yourself into trouble."

I stop and turn toward Tank. "Probably."

He shakes his head. "You need some protection."

"So you'll help me out?" I say. "You think we can find the guy?"

"I think that you, me and Gramps should just leave this alone." He shakes his head. "But I can see there's no way I can convince you of that. So I'll help you. I may know how to find the guy. Give me a day or two."

Chapter Five

"Tommy Park," says Tank. He'd given me a call a couple of days later. Now we're walking south toward Little Korea.

"Where?"

"Not where. Who. Tommy runs a gang."

"You think he did it?"

"Naw. Tommy has too much self-respect to smash and grab like that. But he might know someone. Who'll know someone. Thought you should come with."

We turn down an alley that runs behind a popular takeaway place. An exhaust vent fills the air with the irresistible smell of fried food. We walk past a pile of broken wooden crates. Tank stops in front of a metal fire door.

Tank raps his knuckles sharply on the door. After a moment the door swings open.

"What do you want?" A thin kid in a stained apron appears in the doorway. One of the kitchen staff. Instead of a hairnet, he's wearing a ball cap backward. He's holding a big steel pot, dripping wet. One of the dishwashers.

"Yo, Jin!" says Tank. Big smile.

"What do you want?" Jin repeats. "I'm busy. Lunchtime rush."

"Your uncle around? I need to talk some business."

Jin looks suspicious. But he nods. He gestures for us to come inside.

I find myself in a busy industrial kitchen. It's humid and hot. Big pots of noodles boil endlessly on stainless-steel stoves. A chef tosses around vegetables in a large wok. Flames sizzle up underneath it. I'm distracted by all the action for a moment. Then I realize I don't know which way Tank went.

But I see Jin working over a huge sink, scrubbing something. I wave to get his attention. He doesn't see me. He's got earbuds in. Can't hear me. So I get closer and tap his shoulder. He jumps and spins toward me. Nervous guy.

"What do you want?" he snaps. Up close, I notice he has a cold sore on the edge of his lip. Gross.

I flash back to the robbery. Then back to Jin. I hadn't noticed the logo on his ball cap when he opened the door.

Black Yankees ball cap. Cold sore. Is this the guy?

It's hard to imagine this wiry dishwasher as the burglar. I study his face carefully. Jin seems to pick up on my suspicion. It makes him even more irritated.

"Get out of my face. You shouldn't even be here."

He plants a wet hand on my chest and pushes me back.

I lift my hands up. "Take it easy. I'm just looking for Tank."

Maybe it's the way I hold up my hands. Just like I did during the robbery. Whatever it is, Jin suddenly recognizes me. It *is* him. I see his eyes widen. He plunges his hand into the big sink of dirty dishwater. Then he pulls out a massive knife. He points it at me.

"You followed me here? You call the cops?"

Keeping my hands up, I risk a quick look around. The other chef hasn't noticed what's going on. He's focused on his wok. No sign of Tank. I'm on my own.

"Put that down. I just want to—"

Jin doesn't wait to hear what I have to say. He suddenly swipes with the knife. I feel the blade slide across my left arm but it doesn't break the skin. Stumbling back, I trip and fall to the floor. Jin attacks again, and I roll out of the way.

I reach out and fumble under the stainless steel counter for anything that might help. I come up with a plastic squeeze bottle. It's filled with something red and chunky. Ketchup? Whatever. I squirt. Aiming for Jin's eyes. Direct hit.

Not ketchup. Hot sauce.

Jin screams. He drops the knife so he can rub his eyes with both hands. That makes it worse. He starts screaming even louder.

Which finally attracts the attention of the chef. And a waiter.

And eventually his uncle. Tommy Park. Who is not pleased.

Chapter Six

Pretty soon I'm in a back office with Jin. We're both sitting in beaten-up wooden chairs. Tank leans against the wall to one side. Tommy is behind a huge desk covered in papers. I feel like I'm in the principal's office.

Tommy glares at me. His shaved head reflects the strip lighting above us.

"Tank told me about the robbery. I was genuinely sorry to hear about that. Your grandfather and I worked together. When we were young. Vincent was a great pickpocket. Perhaps the greatest. Never had to use violence. Nobody ever got hurt when he was working. Your grandfather is a good man."

Tommy stands up and crosses in front of the desk. Stands right in front of me, looking down.

"So I was willing to do what I can to help you and your grandfather. But then you pick a fight with my nephew? You cause trouble in my restaurant? My goodwill only goes so far."

"Jin started it," I mutter.

I realize immediately that this is the wrong thing to say. Tommy growls. That can't be good.

"I mean, I think Jin actually did it," I stumble on. "He stole from my grandfather."

"Now you accuse my nephew to get yourself out of trouble?" Tommy's eyes widen. I see muscles around his jaw start to twitch. "Do you know who I am?"

"Whoa, let's slow this all down," says Tank. "Michael, you can't be sure of what you're saying. Don't be throwing accusations around—"

"He's right," says Jin quietly.

Surprised, we all turn toward him. Jin is slumped in his chair. His eyes are puffy and half-closed. His hair is plastered wet to his skull. He nervously fiddles with the ball cap in his lap.

"I robbed the old man," continues Jin. "I didn't know you liked him, uncle! I just picked a place at random."

Tommy and I speak at the same moment. "Why?"

Jin shrugs. And looks even more uncomfortable. "I wanted to impress you, uncle. You never asked me to be part of the business. I wanted to show you I was ready."

"I did not ask you because you are still a child," says Tommy. There's a tightness to his voice. "A child who doesn't know his place in the family."

Jin starts crying again. I can't imagine there are many tears left in him. Not after my hot-sauce attack. But they come streaming down his cheeks. Tommy just shakes his head, looking disgusted.

"Give back whatever you stole," he snaps at Jin.

Jin sniffles. "I can't."

Tommy suddenly looms over him, leaning on the arms of the chair. He snarls, "Do not defy me, boy."

"Uncle, I can't! All I took was a necklace and some cash. And I sold the necklace already. I was going to give you all the money. Here." He reaches into his jeans and pulls out a wad of bills.

Tommy just shakes his head. Then passes the money to me.

"Tank, take your friend and get out. My nephew and I have much to discuss."

Chapter Seven

"I'm sorry. I made it worse. And we didn't find the necklace," I say.

Gramps leans on his cane and moves slowly down the sidewalk. He didn't say a word while I told him the whole story of my adventure with Tank. Now, finally, he turns to me.

"Mikey, Tommy Park is a tough character. Don't stick your nose into his business."

"I'm sorry," I say again.

I expect him to get mad. But Gramps looks at me sadly.

"You shouldn't apologize. This is all my fault. I never should have asked you to help me out. I'm the one who is sorry." He looks at me. Then gives me a hug. He feels thin in my arms. Like a bird.

"What are you going to do now?" I ask.

"Come with me. I have a new plan." We walk until we reach a storefront crowded with gold and silver. Rings and bracelets. The sign above it reads *Crump Antiques and Jewelry*.

A bell tinkles as we walk in. A woman's voice calls from the back of the store that she'll be right out.

"Well, well, well. The Wolf returns!" An older woman with frizzy hair speeds toward Gramps. She wraps him in a bear hug. "Look at you! Still handsome as ever. Why do I never see you around anymore? And who is this striking young man?"

Gramps introduces me. "Mikey, meet Tricia. She used to sell items that I 'acquired.'" He uses air quotes for the last word. "You know, on the job."

Aha. She was his fence, selling stolen goods.

"Is that what brings you here? I thought you retired," says Tricia.

Gramps looks surprised. "You're still buying? I thought you got out of the business a while ago too."

Tricia shrugs. "Sometimes I still move something hot as a favor. Mostly I'm legit. Selling the jewelry that I make." She lifts up her arms to show a tangle of gold and silver bracelets. "They're nice, right?"

"That's why I'm here," says Gramps. "I want you to make me a necklace."

He reaches into his coat and pulls out the picture of him and Grandma on their wedding day. He must have taken it out of the frame. He pulls out a few other photos as well.

"Can you make me a copy of this necklace? I…lost the original. It's important to me," says Gramps.

Tricia has a pair of glasses on a chain around her neck. She puts the glasses on and studies the photos. Then she looks up at Gramps. She has a weird look on her face.

"I had no idea," she says. "No idea. I'm so sorry."

"What are you talking about, Tricia?" says Gramps.

She taps the photo with a long pink fingernail. "I just sold this necklace a couple of days ago. A young guy came in here, saying Tommy Park had sent him. That I should move it fast. He didn't explain where it came from. Just said to sell it quick. As a favor to Tommy."

That must have been Jin. Using his uncle's name to fence the necklace.

"So I found a buyer. Garrett. You know him? Not a nice man. Heard he was involved in moving drugs down at the harbor. Lots of money to throw around. I wouldn't normally deal with someone like that. But the young guy said Tommy wanted it sold fast. So what am I going to do?" She sees Gramps's face. He's gone pale.

"I am so sorry," Tricia repeats. She gently reaches across the counter to put a hand on Gramps's shoulder. "If I had known it was yours, I never would have sold it. What can I do to make it up to you?"

Gramps sighs. "Nothing. Forget about it. It's not your fault. I just to need to let her go." He starts to collect up the photos.

"Wait," I say. I pull out the cash Tommy gave me. "You should have the necklace. Even if it's just a copy." I guess Gramps has forgotten that's why he came in here.

"Tricia, how much will it cost?"

Gramps smiles at me. "Thanks, kiddo."

"Give me a week," says Tricia. "I'll make you one so good you can't tell the difference."

"I'll always know the difference," says Gramps. "But thank you, Tricia."

Chapter Eight

A couple of days later I'm hanging out on the corner with Tank. He's put his usual drumsticks aside while he eats a burrito. The thin tinfoil wrapper barely contains the goopy tortilla.

I've told him all about Tricia. About the original necklace. Gone forever to some big-shot drug dealer. About the copy that Tricia's making.

"How's your Gramps handling it?" Tank asks.

"Not great. I just wish I could have done more, you know?"

"Yeah, I felt the same way," says Tank. "So I asked around. Found out something good."

The bottom of his burrito drops out of the wrapper. Sauce and beans dribble down his hands. His white T-shirt is splattered with burrito juice.

"What did you find out?" I ask. But Tank's concentration is split between the necklace story and his exploding lunch. He doesn't answer. Annoyed, I ask again.

"C'mon—what did you find out?"

"Can't you see I'm in the middle of a crisis?" snaps Tank. "Look at me, man, I'm a mess! And I'm still hungry!"

We're interrupted by a big white van rattling to a stop in front of us. Fancy red letters curl across the side of the van: *Stella's Catering*. The passenger-side window rolls down with a squeak. A young woman leans across from the driver's seat. She's pretty, with dark hair in a ponytail and big hoop earrings.

"Tank! You wearing my food now, you love it so much?"

Despite her teasing, Tank looks relieved instead of annoyed.

"You saved me, Stella! I just wasted one of your finest creations. You have it in your heart to treat me to another one?" Tank is wearing his widest smile.

Stella just shakes her head. "Get in, you charmer."

Tank happily opens the door and climbs into the van. What's he doing?

"Wait, Tank—you're just leaving me here? I need to find out—"

Tank rolls his eyes. "What you need is a good meal. Get in."

He leans back, and the rear door to the big van slides open. I clamber inside. The van is a little kitchen on wheels. It's stuffed with shining stainless-steel shelves. Containers of ingredients. A little stove and fridge toward the back. There's a small pull-down seat on one wall, behind the driver. I sit down and buckle up as Stella pulls away from the corner.

"Stella, meet Michael," says Tank.

"Tank told me all about you," says Stella as she navigates the van through the city streets. "Told me about your Gramps. He sounds like a sweetheart. Looking for his beloved wife's necklace and all."

Tank rustles around in a container at his feet, then tosses a paper bag of fried tortilla chips back to me. They smell great. They taste even better. Stella keeps talking as she drives.

"So when Tank told me about everything,

I realized I might know the guy who bought the necklace. Hang on—I've got to merge to get onto the bridge." Traffic thickens around the van as we leave downtown.

Tank jumps in to tell the rest of the story. "So this guy hires Stella a couple of weeks ago. His wife loves throwing parties. Well, Jenna is his third wife. Half his age. A million times better-looking than her husband. Bradley Garrett."

"Wait," I say. "Garrett—the same guy Tricia sold the necklace to?"

"Same one," says Tank. We've picked up speed now. This is a nice part of town. Big houses. Wide green lawns. Hedges and fences to keep everyone out.

"The party is tomorrow night," says Stella.

"Tank asked me if you guys could tag along. I'm meeting with Jenna now. Maybe you can talk to her? See if she'd be willing to part with it?"

"What's the worst that can happen?" says Tank. "She says no. We go home."

Chapter Nine

Stella pulls the van up to a big gate. She leans toward a metal box and punches a button.

"I'm here to meet with Mrs. Garrett," she says. After a moment the gate whirs open. The van crunches along a gravel driveway. The house is massive. Windows with black shutters stare at us from above. The lawn around the house is trimmed perfectly. Like a golf course. I've seen mansions like this on TV. I wasn't actually sure they existed in real life.

Stella parks the van, and we all pile out. A young woman comes down the front steps to meet us. Like Tank said, Jenna doesn't look much older than us. Black hair falls loose around her face, which is covered by huge sunglasses. Her blue dress looks like something a model would wear.

The necklace she's wearing looks great with the outfit.

Grandma's necklace.

"You're a little late, Stella," says Jenna with a tight smile. "Not really what I want from my caterer."

"Sorry, I just had to pick up some—" Stella hesitates. She stares at me, unsure what to say.

"You had to pick up your staff. I'm a cook." I turn to Tank. "And this is our...head waiter."

Tank shoots me a frustrated look. Like, why is he waiter and I'm a cook? Stella plays along.

"Well, all right," says Jenna. "Follow me. I'll show you where we'll set everything up." She leads us through the house. It's amazing. All white and glass. Antiques and expensive art are carefully arranged on every wall. We walk through an entrance hall into a lounge. Then through big glass doors onto a pool deck. The pool shimmers like a small blue ocean.

"We'll have about a hundred guests on Friday," says Jenna. "The kitchen is right over there. I have some ideas about the appetizers." She starts to rattle off a list. I just nod like I've heard it all before. Meanwhile I'm studying the necklace. That's definitely the one from the pictures. Suddenly I realize that Jenna just asked me a question. Something about fish and crackers. Maybe.

"Sorry, I was distracted by your necklace," I say. "It's really nice."

Jenna looks both confused and a little flattered. "Um, thank you? But I asked you about the salmon…"

"Sure, sure. It's really nice too. Before we get to that, do you mind my asking where you got that necklace? It reminds me of one my grandmother had."

Jenna's confusion makes her babble. "Really? Uh, Bradley bought it for me last week. An anniversary present. He said it was a very rare antique. I wouldn't normally wear it just around, you know?" One of her elegant hands reaches up to cover the necklace protectively. "Could we please stick to talking about the food? This feels awkward."

"Of course," says Stella. "Let me tell you all about my special spicy sauce." The two of them move away from us and the pool.

"That woman doesn't know she's wearing stolen goods," says Tank. "But she'd never believe us if we told her."

"Nope. I don't think I could buy it off her either. Money isn't a thing for someone like her."

Tank and I watch Stella and Jenna walk across the perfect lawn. Jenna is gesturing, pointing out where tents and tables will go. The sunlight catches on the necklace as she turns. It flares like a little star.

"So that's it. We're out of options," says Tank.

I look at the massive house. The tall hedge around the edge of the property. I see two little black boxes mounted on poles. Security cameras. Designed to keep people out. But there's not much to stop someone if they are already inside. A plan starts to form in my mind. I pull out my phone. Pretending to be texting, I start taking pictures of the house. The security cameras. Trying to memorize the layout.

"I think we've got one more option, Tank. It's a little crazy, but it might work."

Chapter Ten

Gramps is furious.

"Your plan isn't just crazy. It's ridiculous. There is no way that this will work!" He's yelling. I've never heard Gramps yell before. He gets up from the couch, where I've just told him about my plan. He starts pacing around his apartment. Shuffling with his cane.

"Hang on, Gramps. Maybe I didn't explain it right. Let me try again," I say. "It starts with Stella picking us up from the corner of Becker and Key at six o'clock tonight. She brings us to the party. Jenna already thinks we work with her."

"And Jenna's already suspicious of you! Right there, your plan is cooked. You're done!" Gramps thwacks the floor with his cane for emphasis.

I pinch the bridge of my nose. I've got a headache coming on. "Okay, maybe. Maybe not. Stella is bringing some other staff. I think we'll just kind of blend in. Tank and I will keep it low-key."

Gramps snorts. "Tank has his nickname for a reason, kiddo. He's not exactly subtle."

I keep going with the plan. "Anyways, once the party is really busy, Tank and I will head upstairs. Jenna said she didn't normally wear the necklace. So she'll probably keep it in her bedroom. Which I'm pretty sure is upstairs, because I didn't see it on the ground floor."

"And if someone catches you strolling around?"

"We just say that we got lost. We're looking for the bathroom. Or something."

"That's a terrible line." Gramps stops pacing. "This is all my fault. I never should have asked you to help."

"Gramps, I can do this. You did this kind of stuff your entire life, right? Tommy said you were the greatest thief ever. This is an easy job compared to what you did."

"And I ended up in jail!" yells Gramps.

His voice is getting hoarse from shouting. "Does that not teach you anything? I thought you were smart, Mikey. Learn the lesson here!" His face suddenly drains of color. He puts a hand on his chest and takes a deep breath.

"Gramps, calm down! Remember your heart condition! Should I get your pills?"

Gramps has gone from furious to exhausted. He just…deflates. I ease him down onto the couch.

After a moment Gramps pulls out an envelope from his pocket and opens it. Then carefully takes out a necklace. The copy Tricia made for him.

"Mikey, all I've got now is this copy. I know it's not the real thing. And I admit, it kills me that a scumbag like Bradley Garrett has the real one."

"Right," I say. "I won't feel bad about stealing from that guy. Tricia said Bradley is a big-time drug dealer. And I'm just taking back what's yours."

Gramps fixes me with his fiercest wolflike stare. "You will do no such thing. Michael, I'm telling you. Stay out of this. It's not your business. I never should have involved you. You're not up for this. Go home. And stay home."

His words snap out like bullets. He's never talked to me this way.

"You want me gone?" I say.

"Stay out of my business, kiddo," he says. Tired but firm. "You're just a child."

Fine.

As I walk down Becker Street toward the pick-up point, I make a decision. Gramps is wrong. I can do this. I'm not going to let people like Jin and Bradley get away with it. Sure, I'm going to have to do some things that are wrong. But the reasons feel right.

Chapter Eleven

To start, everything goes according to plan. Tank and I look good in our uniforms. Stella dug up some white shirts, black pants and jackets for us. Just like the rest of her catering staff wear. Until the guests arrive, I stay in the kitchen. Stirring pots, chopping vegetables. Whatever

Stella tells me to do. Mainly I avoid being seen by Jenna.

Tank roams around though. He's charming as a waiter. I think Stella should actually hire him.

Finally Tank comes and taps me on the shoulder. "It's time. There's a big enough crowd out there. They won't notice us."

I take off my apron and put on a thin black jacket. Now my uniform looks just like Tank's. We move to the sliding doors that open to the outside. The crowd covers the lawn. Well-dressed people stand along the edge of the pool. The lights reflect off the water onto their expensive clothes. Gentle music floats through the air. I spot Stella talking to Jenna near a table decorated with an ice sculpture. I hustle past the door, hoping we're not spotted.

Once we're in the entrance hallway, we have to stop. A couple walks through the front door. Tank acts like he was waiting there all along to greet them.

"Welcome to the Garretts'! The party is straight through there, by the pool. May I take your jacket?"

The man shrugs off his jacket and hands it to me.

"You got a cloakroom or something?" he asks. The jacket feels expensive. He gives me his name.

"Of course, sir," I say. I try to sound like a butler. It seems to work. The couple follows the sound of laughter and music into the next room. We're alone again. I carefully lay the jacket on a low bench.

"You're not going to check the pockets?" asks Tank. "Might be something nice in there. Cash? Fancy phone? A little bonus for us, that's all."

"What? No! We're just here to get the necklace," I say. I start to climb the stairs to the second floor. "I'm not a thief, Tank."

Tank raises an eyebrow, then follows me.

At the top of the stairs, we can go left or right. I pull out my phone and flip through the pictures I took the day before. I'm pretty sure some sort of office is to the right. So bedrooms are probably on the left. Which is where we go.

After two tries we find the master bedroom. It's massive. Everything in white and brown. A huge bed the size of a small island. A hot tub near the window, overlooking the pool.

"Tank, you're on lookout," I say quietly. He keeps the door cracked barely open and peers out through the slit.

I scan the room. The vanity loaded with glass bottles and shiny boxes. That's where I start.

Turns out I'm better at robbery than Jin was. I quickly find a fancy box in a drawer. I open it up. Rings, bracelets and necklaces gleam up at me.

But not the one I'm looking for. Not my grandmother's necklace.

I hear a low whistle behind me.

"You sure we can't take a few of these things? Just a little extra payment?" says Tank. He's leaning over my shoulder. Staring at all the gold and silver. "She won't notice anything is missing. Look at all this!"

"Tank!" I hiss. "Get back on lookout! You're supposed to be over there!" I point toward the door.

And watch as the heavy wooden door slowly eases open. A black, wet nose appears. Followed by a black-and-brown dog. He pushes his way into the room. Then freezes when he sees us.

Like everything else in this house, the dog is huge. His thick head comes up to my chest.

The dog growls. Low and steady. The sound reminds me of Tommy Park. Same kind of growl.

I feel the same kind of fear.

Chapter Twelve

Surprisingly, Tank moves slowly toward the dog.

"What are you doing?" I whisper. "Are you crazy?"

"Shut up," Tank says quietly to me. Then, to the dog, "Who's a good puppy? Who's a hungry puppy?"

The dog's ears flick backward. It lowers itself toward the floor. Like a spring coiling up. Ready to launch. But Tank keeps his voice calm and steady.

"Who's a hungry puppy?" he repeats. Tank slowly pulls something wrapped in tinfoil from his pocket. "Who wants one of Stella's magic burritos?"

The dog sniffs. Uncoils a little. Tank unwraps the burrito and puts it carefully on the white carpet. Then takes a step back. The big dog eases toward the food. Sniffs again.

Then attacks it. Sauce and meat splatter across the carpet.

"I packed a snack." Tank smiles at me. "Such a shame to waste it on the puppy." We quickly skirt around the dog, who ignores us as it feasts on the burrito. Closing the bedroom door behind us, we hustle back down the stairs.

"So what now?" asks Tank as we walk.

"I don't know," I say. "This wasn't the way it was supposed to work." As we head back toward the kitchen, Stella rushes through one of the doors.

"There you are. You've got a problem," she says. "Actually, two problems."

We follow her toward the party. The crowd has gotten even bigger and noisier.

"Problem number one," says Stella. There's Jenna, ten feet away. Laughing with Bradley.

"I don't get it," I say.

"Look at what she's wearing," says Stella. "That's it, isn't it?"

Oh no. Jenna decided to wear the necklace tonight.

"Then what's problem number two?" I ask.

Stella points, trying to keep it subtle.

"He is," she says. "That's your Gramps, right?"

It's him, all right. Standing right at the edge of the pool. Looking good in a sharp suit. A hat just like gangsters in movies used to wear. Leaning on his cane with one hand. He's scanning the crowd. Like a wolf looking for prey.

I walk over to him as fast as I can without attracting attention.

"What are you doing here?" I hiss.

Gramps's smile doesn't change. "Mikey! I knew you'd try to pull this off. I appreciate your loyalty. Your dedication. You are a wonderful grandson," he says. "But I'll take it from here. I'm just going to have a word with Mr. and Mrs. Garrett."

"What are you talking about? Gramps, I promised Mom I'd keep you safe. That guy is bad news. You've got to go home—"

"I don't think so." Gramps just shakes his head. "Also, and I mean this, you should think about a career in medicine. As a criminal, you don't have a future." As I stand there, speechless, he starts to shuffle toward Jenna and Bradley. I look over at Tank and Stella and shrug. My plan is in shreds. I've never seen Gramps like this. I think he's losing it.

Just as Gramps gets close to Jenna, he drops his cane. His eyes widen. He lets out a low moan and clutches his chest. Stumbling, he crashes into Bradley. Bounces off of him. Into the arms of Jenna. Gramps grasps at her.

"Please," he croaks. "Help me."

Gramps!

Jenna, cradling Gramps, looks around frantically.

"Is anyone a doctor?" she asks. "I think this man is having a heart attack!"

I'm not a doctor, but Mom taught me what to do if Gramps has an attack. I rush to her side and gently take Gramps in my arms and ease him to the ground.

"Do you have your pills with you?" I ask.

Gramps's eyes roll back into his head. "Inside jacket," he mutters.

I reach inside his suit jacket and pull out a medicine bottle. I take two white pills and press them under his tongue. Just like Mom taught me to do.

Jenna leans over. I see the necklace gleaming against her skin. "Will he be all right?" she asks.

I don't care about the necklace anymore. All I want is for Gramps to be okay.

I can't speak without crying. So I just shake my head in answer to her.

The crowd is quiet. Everyone is waiting to see what will happen.

Gramps's eyes flutter open. He focuses on me.

"Mikey," he says with a weak smile. "You saved me, kiddo," he says quietly.

Chapter Thirteen

Stella had called 9-1-1 when Gramps went down. Tank and Stella move us out of the way to wait for the ambulance. Behind us, Jenna resumes her hostess duties. Stella goes back to work, Tank following behind to help. The noise of the party builds up again as everyone moves on from the excitement.

Gramps and I sit on a low bench outside the front door, alone.

"I'm so sorry," I say. "You were right. I never should have stuck my nose in any of this. I just made it all worse."

Gramps leans against me. He feels light, like a good gust of wind might blow him away. "I said it before—you've got nothing to be sorry for," he says. "And I'm glad you were there for me."

"But this is all my fault. You nearly died. And we still don't have the necklace."

"Well...that's not entirely true," says Gramps. He reaches into his suit pocket and pulls out the pendant.

"Yeah, but that's just the copy," I say. "Jenna still has the original."

"That's what she thinks. But this one is the real thing," he says with a wink. "When the charming Mrs. Garrett was helping me off the ground, I swapped them on her."

"Wait," I say. "You were in the middle of a heart attack! And you still managed to scam her?"

Gramps snorts. "Like Tommy said, I'm the best in the business. To be fair, poor Jenna was quite distracted. I feel a little bad about it. But now she has Tricia's excellent copy. She'll never know the difference. And those pills you slipped me were mints. I'm fine."

Whoa. Gramps had it all worked out. He was several steps ahead of all of us the whole time. I see the red and white flashing lights of the ambulance in the distance.

A siren gets louder as it approaches the house. I wonder what we'll tell the paramedics. *Thanks anyway, but this was all just part of a finely executed heist.*

"One more thing," Gramps says. "This was my last job. I mean it. No more stealing. I got what I wanted, and I'm done. But this was *your* last job too. You understand? This was your first and last shot at being a criminal."

"Yeah," I say. "You're right. I should probably go into medicine. Mom would sure be happy." I place my hand on his shoulder. "It's too bad though, Gramps. We made a good team."

Gramps and I smile at each other.

Like a pair of wolves.

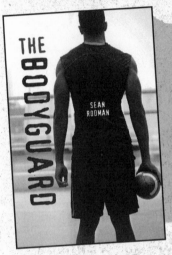

Dylan struggles with the memories of the death of his younger brother while fighting for survival in a snow-bound resort.

"Fast-paced and intense."
—CM Magazine

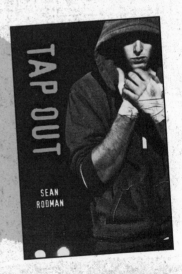

Darwin is sent to an exclusive new school for a fresh start from the violent influence of his father. But old habits die hard, and Darwin ends up in an illegal fight club.

"A knock out!"
—Resource Links

Sean Rodman is the author of several books for young people, including *The Bodyguard* and *Firewall* in the Orca Soundings line. When not working on his own books, Sean is the executive director of the Story Studio, a charity that inspires, educates and empowers youth to be great storytellers. He lives in Victoria, British Columbia.

For more information on all the books

in the Orca Anchor line, please visit

orcabook.com